# There Goes the Wind

## By Riley Esposito

Copyright © 2022 Riley Esposito.
All rights reserved.
Published by Riley Esposito

978-1-387-89879-4
Imprint: Lulu.com

To my dog, Cindy, who kept me positive while friend searching.

**Prologue**

I always stand in the middle of the recess field, letting Wind blow me every which way. Wind is my friend. No, it's my best friend. The good thing about having Wind as your friend is that no matter where you go, Wind is always with you. In the car you could open a window. Even when you go into a store, you know how a gust of wind blows in with you as you open the door? That's my friend, Wind. He's always there, right by my side. No matter what mood I'm in, Wind knows exactly how to express it. When I'm in a bad mood, Wind blows the rain and trees outside. When I'm stressed, Wind blows in my face and makes me feel relaxed. That's what I like. That's how I know it's my best friend, Wind.

# Chapter One

"Jack," my mama said, unlocking the car door. When she did I jumped in and opened the window right away. Wind blew into the car. I smiled. "You need to find some real friends. Some friends that are actually physical," mama finished. I sighed. This was about the millionth time my mama was having this conversation with me.

"I'm fine, mama. Wind can keep me plenty of company," I assured her. Mama sighed again. I rolled my eyes. "Can you believe she doesn't think you're a real friend?" I thought to Wind. "Yeah, I can't believe it either," Wind told me. When he replied I knew it was him.

It was like Wind and I had a special language only we could understand. Mama drove me to school. I'm in the second grade, which means next year I'll be in third. I know Wind is my best friend, but I do have another friend that's in third grade. His name is Ben. My mama almost always forgets his name. He's always scared when I mention fourth grade, because he says the teacher for fourth grade is really strict. I try to comfort him, but to be honest, it sometimes scares me too. I got out of the car with mama.

"Maybe you should try to talk to your friend today. What's his name? Brad?" Mama said.

I rolled my eyes again. "Mama, it's Ben," I corrected.

"Silly me," she said. Before I walked into school, mama pulled me aside. "Make room to make new friends today," she said and kissed me on my forehead. I nodded my head and walked into school.

When I pushed open the heavy glass door to get inside the school, Wind blew in with me. "I still don't understand why *she* can't understand that you're a real friend," I thought to Wind. Wind rolled his eyes. "I wonder that sometimes as well. She can be so clueless," Wind said. "Tell me about it." Wind and I arrived to class.

My teacher, Miss Franny, was sitting at her desk. Her pointy nose was in a book, and her glasses were just balancing on the tip of it. Her eyes were narrowed and her blond hair was tied up in a strict looking bun. Miss Franny wasn't as strict as she looked, but she could definitely yell when she wanted to. I unpacked my backpack (which was a really nice shade of dark blue) and sat down at my desk. Wind sat right next to me. And that's where he was the rest of the day.

## Chapter Two

"Get everything you need for lunch and recess and then line up at the door," Miss Franny said. The girls went to grab jump ropes and chalk to play tic-tac-toe. The boys grabbed a ball to play kickball. I didn't need anything for recess, because I had my best friend Wind there, right next to me. I went outside and let Wind push me all about.

Then it was time to go back inside so we lined up by the gate. There, another boy in my class came up to me. He was a new boy that just started last week. He smiled a big, wide, friendly smile. He stuck his hand out at me.

"Hi, my name is Marc! What's yours? Do you want to be friends?" the boy said.

I looked at him until a smile spread across my face, which didn't take long. "My name is Jack. And sure, I would love to be friends!" I replied.

Marc and I talked during lunch. We talked while leaving school.

"See you tomorrow, Jack!" Marc said, waving as he left to get to his mama's car. "See ya!" I replied and waved. I thought about my mama, and what she said before I went to school that day.

"*Make room to make new friends today,*" she had said. I smiled at myself. I think I did just that.

"And Marc and I talked about which toppings on pizza were better, and we both agreed that pepperoni and meatballs are the best ones," I told mama. The only part of mama I could see was the back of her head, but even from there I could tell she was smiling.

"I'm glad you listened to what I said and made a new friend," she said.

There was only one problem that I had to solve. And it was a scary kind of problem. I needed to tell Wind about Marc, unless he already knew about it since he followed me and Marc back into the school.

When we got home and I finished my homework, I went outside in my backyard to tell Wind. I didn't feel him come through the door with me when I went inside the house earlier. "Wind," I thought to him, "I know you're upset at me because I met Marc, but you know you'll always be my friend." Wind didn't respond. He only blew one big blow of Wind at my face, and then I couldn't feel him anymore. Where had he gone? Did he leave? Is he going to be with another second grader? And then leave once the second grader found a nice friend like Marc? I repeated these questions to my mama that night. She sighed a long sigh. "All we can do is hope," was her reply. "All we can do is hope."

## Chapter Three

The next day I couldn't feel any Wind. Was Wind really gone? Did he really leave me to go with another second grader? During recess I told my problem to Ben and Marc.

"Hmm," they both said. I looked from Ben's face to Marc's face, repeatedly until I saw a look on Ben's face that looked like he had an idea.

"What is it?" I asked eagerly.

"Oh, never mind. That would never work," he said, his face falling. I sighed the same type of sigh my mama sighed the other night.

"Maybe he just wanted to give you a boost. You know, to find friends and not be lonely. I used to be friends with Wind when I was three," Marc said and held up three fingers.

I looked at him with thoughtful eyes. Wind never told me he was with other kids before. I thought I was his first kid.

"When I was three, I didn't have much of a knack for making friends," Marc continued. "But then Wind told me that he would be my friend. So me and Wind would always play and hang out during school and at home. It was always like we had this secret language only me and him understood."

What Marc was saying sounded like my friendship with Wind, at least what it used to be.

"Until one day at preschool I made a friend, James. From then on, Wind never visited me again. But now I'm happy, and have all my friends, like Jack," Marc pointed to me. I smiled.

"And Ben." He pointed to Ben.

"And I'm still friends with James. I also have many other

friends." Marc smiled as he finished his story.

"So... Wind's really gone?" I asked, unsure.

Marc nodded. "I'm sorry," Ben said, almost in a whisper.

I'm kinda sorry for me as well.

## Chapter Four

I was sad the rest of the day. When I got home I threw my backpack on the floor and went outside immediately. I went to see if Wind would come back. Who cares what Marc says? Who cares what happened to him when he was three years old? What if he was lying? I know Wind and I know he wouldn't just leave me like that. I went outside. No breeze. No Wind. I did my homework outside. I chewed on my eraser, too nervous to do my math. I just wanted Wind back.

"Jack, you need to come in. It's dark outside and it's time for bed," mama said when it was my bedtime at eight o'clock.

I shook my head. "No, mama. I refuse," I replied. "I want, no need, to stay outside and see if Wind comes back."

Mama shook her head at me. "Alright, Jack, if that's what you really want," she said and went back inside.

As I watched the lights inside turn off until the whole house was dark, a creepy feeling suddenly came over me. I frantically pried the handle of the door to the inside of the house and ran inside. I slept with my mama that night. It was a scary night. I blame Wind for everything that happened outside.

# Chapter Five

It's been a week without my friend Wind, but now I have a whole group to hang out with at recess! Marc introduced me to his friend, Lisa, so now we have a girl in the group! She's really cool! Every Friday after school, after we all finish our homework, we all play this really fun video game we love! We talk during lunch and play during recess. Wind still comes by once in a while, but he never talks. I think he might have forgotten about our secret language. But that's okay, because I have new friends! I have Lisa, Marc, and Ben!

"Hang on guys, let me just get my lunchbox!" I called to

them as I ran over to a wooden table on the field one day at recess. I stopped for a moment. I felt Wind coming. But this time I heard him speaking. Maybe he didn't forget the secret language!

"Jack," Wind called. "I was there for you when you didn't have friends, and I want you to know that even though I may be leaving," he took a long pause, "I'll always be there for you in the future."

I felt a big blow of Wind pass by me. Like he said, even though he may be leaving, I know what he said was true. I know. I know because he's the best friend anyone will ever have.

# The End

Made in the USA
Coppell, TX
24 July 2022